Twilight Chant

by HOLLY THOMPSON

illustrated by JEN BETTON

CLARION BOOKS

Houghton Mifflin Harcourt
Boston   New York

Clarion Books
3 Park Avenue
New York, New York 10016

Clarion Books is an imprint of Houghton Mifflin Harcourt Publishing Company.

hmhco.com

The illustrations in this book were done in
watercolor with colored pencil and pastel on Strathmore 500 board.
The text was set in Brioso Pro.

Library of Congress Cataloging-in-Publication Data
Names: Thompson, Holly, author. | Betton, Jen, illustrator.
Title: Twilight chant / Holly Thompson ; illustrations by Jen Betton.
Description: Boston ; New York : Clarion Books, Houghton Mifflin Harcourt,
[2018] | Audience: Age 4-7. | Summary: As twilight falls, some animals
come out to graze while others are settling in for the night.
Identifiers: LCCN 2016058568 | ISBN 9780544586482 (hardcover)
Subjects: LCSH: Nocturnal animals—Juvenile literature. | Animal behavior—Juvenile literature.
Classification: LCC QL755.5 .T46 2018 | DDC [E]—dc23
LC record available at https://lccn.loc.gov/2016058568

Manufactured in China
SCP 10 9 8 7 6 5 4 3 2 1
4500689137

For my parents, who fostered a love of nature
—H.T.

For Ella, who was patient, and Claire, my production baby
—J.B.

In the twilight
the low light
the sun has just gone down light

play is done
  start for home
    as clouds begin to glow in the

twilight
  the low light
    the egrets fly to roost light

find a tree
      preen, clean
          hide inside your wings in the

      twilight
       the low light
         the swallows start to feed light

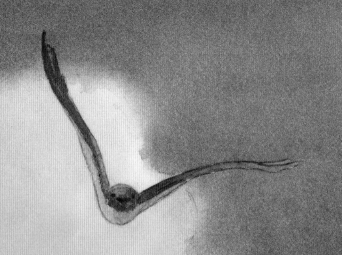

swerve up
   wing low
      skim above the fields in the

twilight
   the low light
      the deer come out to graze light

meadow's edge
　forest glade
　　watch out for coyotes! in the

　twilight
　　the low light
　　　the bats all swoop and swerve light

zoom high
sonar in
eat whatever flies in the

twilight
the low light
the rabbits hop about light

find a thicket
    follow fencerow
        nibble, then be still! in the

    twilight
        the low light
            the foxes leave their den light

trot trot
jump walls
sniff out birds and voles in the

twilight
the low light
the fireflies turn bright light

blink, wait
  signal mates
   flicker on and off in the

      twilight
       the low light
        the skunks slink over lawn light

dig a hole
  grubs and worms
    scratch a hive for bees in the

  twilight
    the low light
      the june bugs start to buzz light

beat your wings
   pilot up
      find some leaves to munch in the

twilight
  the low light
    the cats stretch out their legs light

prowl slow
pounce fast
try to catch some mice in the

twilight
the low light
the windows light up gold light

night sight
    takes time
        wait and soon you'll see in the

    twilight
        the low light
            the early evening half-light

before night
the magic light
the creeping dusk of twilight

About Twilight

Twilight is the time of low or "half" light after sunset and before sunrise. During twilight, the sun is below the horizon, but the sky is still bright.

The duration of twilight is longest around the time of the summer and winter solstices and shortest around the time of the spring and fall equinoxes. Twilight also lasts longer closer to the earth's poles. In areas located far north or far south of the equator, around the time of the summer solstice, twilight can last from sunset until sunrise.

Most animals are either diurnal—mainly active during the day—or nocturnal—mainly active at night. But some animals are crepuscular (from the Latin word *crepusculum*, meaning "dusk" or "twilight"). Crepuscular animals are mainly active during twilight.

In the twilight hours, many nocturnal or diurnal animals do not see well, and crepuscular species may have adapted to feed when predators are at a disadvantage. Some animals, though, such as coyotes, may emerge at twilight to feed on crepuscular animals.

This book includes some of the most visible animals active at twilight in North America. Other crepuscular animals in North America include opossum, moose, and various invertebrates (some moths and beetles). Egrets and herons, though not crepuscular, can be seen returning to roost in their nesting colonies at evening twilight.

Animals in order of appearance

EGRETS	RABBITS	SKUNKS
SWALLOWS	FOX	JUNE BUGS
DEER	FIREFLIES	(OR JUNE BEETLES)
BATS		CAT